W9-CCY-352

That New Baby!

By Patricia Relf

Illustrated by DyAnne DiSalvo

A GOLDEN BOOK • New York
Western Publishing Company, Inc.
Racine, Wisconsin 53404

Copyright © 1980 by Western Publishing Company, Inc. All rights reserved. Printed in the U.S.A. No part of this book may be reproduced or copied in any form without written permission from the publisher. GOLDEN®, GOLDEN & DESIGN®, A GOLDEN STORYTIME BOOK®, and A GOLDEN BOOK® are trademarks of Western Publishing Company, Inc. Library of Congress Catalog Card Number: 80-50286 ISBN 0-307-11989-0
PQRST

Elizabeth had a new baby brother. When Mommy and
Daddy brought him home from the hospital, Elizabeth
was waiting on the porch with Grandma.

What a fuss everyone made over that new baby!
Grandma gave him a bunny cup.

"I don't know why," thought Elizabeth. "He can't
drink out of a cup yet."

Aunt Nancy gave him a teddy bear
with a wind-up music box inside.
Uncle George took lots of pictures.
"I don't know why," thought Elizabeth.
"All Mikey ever does is eat and
sleep and cry."

At first Mikey cried a lot! Mommy and Daddy took turns getting up at night to give him his bottle.

Sometimes Elizabeth asked Daddy to bring her a drink, too.
He didn't mind . . . once in a while.

When Mikey was old enough to go places, Elizabeth liked being a big sister.

She liked teaching Mikey how to say "doggy!"

She liked helping him
learn to walk.

And it was fun when Mikey
learned to throw a ball.

But most of the time Elizabeth thought Mikey was just a lot of trouble.

He made a mess when he ate his cereal.

His diaper always needed changing.

And Elizabeth had to walk around on tiptoe whenever Mikey took a nap.

But sometimes Daddy read to Elizabeth while Mikey slept.

One day, while Mommy was resting, Elizabeth decided to give Mikey a special treat. She brought out her favorite toy— a racing car set.

She set up the tracks inside Mikey's playpen.
Mikey looked a little bit worried.
"On your mark, get set, *go!*" said Elizabeth.

VROOOOOOM! went the racing car.
"Waaaaaaaaaaaah!" cried Mikey.

"Coming!" Mommy called.
"Oh, oh," said Elizabeth.

"Elizabeth!" shouted Mommy crossly. "This toy could hurt Mikey. Whatever were you thinking of? Pick up that car and take it to your room. Right now!"

Elizabeth marched to her room and slammed the door.

"I hate being a big sister, and I hate that dumb baby!" Elizabeth shouted.

"I'm going to stay in my room . . . for always!"

Mommy and Daddy came
a little later and knocked on
Elizabeth's door: "May Daddy
and I come in?" Mommy
asked.

"NO!" shouted Elizabeth.

Elizabeth stayed in her
room for the rest of the day.

She played with her
racing car.

She played with her
dollhouse.
But after a while she
began feeling lonely.

She wished she hadn't
shouted at Mommy.

Then, suddenly, Elizabeth
heard Mikey crying.
"Elizabeth!" called Mommy.
"Can you look in on Mikey?"

Elizabeth forgot that she was angry and ran to Mikey's room.

Poor Mikey! He was awfully upset. He was probably feeling as lonely as Elizabeth.

But Elizabeth knew just what to do. She made a funny face and Mikey stopped crying.